FLUFFY AND THE PLATINUM JUBILEE

By
Joshua, Joseph
And James Grant

Published by Grant Publishing

Sales and Enquires: grantpublishingltd@gmail.com

Dedicated to

OUR LOVELY GRANDPARENTS

Fluffy loves to eat carrots
and grass that is green
But most of all
Fluffy loves The Queen

She had pictures of the palace
On her bedroom walls
And would wear her sparkly tiara
When she answered calls

She would read about
the Commonwealth
Which was always fun
And would drink tea with
a raised pinkie
Until she was done.

This year was even more
special
Fluffy was filled with
excitement and glee
It is because
It is Queen's platinum
Jubilee

Fluffy packed her bags
And was heading to London
Town
She wanted to meet the
Queen in person
And catch a glimpse of the
Crown.

She hopped on a train

Which was very fast

She was so excited

She nearly missed the

'You've arrived at London'

broadcast

It was 2pm in the afternoon
Fluffy had finally arrived
'London is very busy'
Fluffy said sounding surprised

There were cars and buses
Everywhere Fluffy looked
'Now let's find The Palace'
Fluffy said as she opened her
travel book

Fluffy jumped on a bus
Which took her to many different places
She saw some famous landmarks
And even more faces.

Oxford Circus and The Gherkin

Are some of the places she saw

As she got closer to the Palace

Her excitement grew even more.

From a distance
Fluffy could see Palace
Guards
Which meant she would
arrive at the Palace
In just a few yards.

Fluffy reached the Palace
gates
And the Guards greeted her
'I'm here to see the Queen'
Nervous Fluffy whispered

'Well I'm afraid
The Queen is very busy today
Her Platinum Jubilee parade
Is hours away'

'So please Rabbit
Be on your way.
You can come back
Another day'.

Fluffy was disappointed
'I guess it time to go home
I am not going to meet The
Queen
Or see her throne'.

Fluffy hopped on a bus home
And while inside
She saw a little woman
Having a carriage ride

Fluffy looked a little closer
and realised that it was The
Queen
It was the most glorious sight
She had ever seen

Fluffy jumped off the bus
And rushed to the Queen
'Hello your majesty
How have you been?'

'Good day dear
How do you do?
I'm Elizabeth the Queen
What say you?'

'My name is Fluffy, Your Majesty
I am your biggest fan!'
Fluffy smiled her widest smile
Everything had gone to plan!

'Why thank you dear
Unfortunately I must flee
I must hurry to the parade
for my platinum Jubilee'

Fluffy stayed and enjoyed
The Platinum Jubilee celebrations
There was a parade and a pageant
What a wonderful occasion.

Printed in Great Britain
by Amazon

79791953R00016